Too Hot For Ice Cream

Too Hot For Ice Cream

by Jean Van Leeuwen
Pictures by Martha Alexander

The Dial Press / New York

E
VAN

Library of Congress Cataloging in Publication Data
Van Leeuwen, Jean. Too hot for ice cream.
[1. City and town life—Fiction]
I. Alexander, Martha G., illus. II. Title.
PZ7.V275To [E] 74-2877
ISBN 0-8037-6076-0 / ISBN 0-8037-6077-9 (lib. bdg.)

For David and Elizabeth

Oh, it was hot.

Sara blew the damp bangs off her forehead. She was sitting on the stoop outside her apartment house waiting for Daddy. He was coming to take her and her sister Elizabeth swimming. But Daddy was late.

Sara looked toward the end of the block. No rattly old gray convertible was turning the corner. Hardly anything at all was moving on Sara's block. It was too hot.

Down the street old Mrs. Maloney sat in her window slowly fanning herself: flip-flop, flip-flop. On the next-door stoop Mr. Greene and Mr. Levine were playing chess. But neither of them had made a move for a long time. Even Mr. Levine's dog Alice wasn't barking at everything as she usually did. She lay across the step like a floppy toy dog with her tongue hanging out.

"Sara."

It was her mother, standing in the open window. "Daddy's on the phone. He wants to talk to you."

Sara stood up. Daddy was calling to say he was going to be late. But Sara already knew that.

"Eee-*anhh*, eee-*anhh*."

Inside Elizabeth was riding her motorcycle around and around the coffee table, making a sound like an ambulance. Sara's mother didn't seem to notice. She was sitting on the floor staring at the typewriter. When she was writing a poem, Sara's mother didn't notice anything.

"Be quiet, Elizabeth, it's Daddy," Sara said. "Hi, Daddy," she said into the phone.

"Hi, Pumpkin," said Daddy's voice. He sounded hot and far away. "I've got bad news. The car wouldn't start and I had to have it towed to a garage. I don't know when it will be fixed. So it looks like no beach today. But we'll go next Saturday instead, okay?"

"Sure, Daddy." Sara tried not to sound as sad as she felt inside. After all, it wasn't Daddy's fault. "I hope the car is fixed soon. Bye, Daddy."

"See you tomorrow. Hug Elizabeth for me."

Sara sat with her chin in her hands. Why did the dumb old car have to pick the hottest day of the summer not to start? It wasn't fair.

Sara's mother's fingers were going peck-peck on the typewriter key Sara waited until they stopped.

"Mama?"

"Hmmmm? Oh, what did Daddy want, honey?"

"The car won't go so he can't take us to the beach. Can you take us, Mama?"

Sara's mother looked at the typewriter and then at Sara. "Oh, honey, it's too hot to go swimming. You know how long that subway ride is. Besides, I want to finish this poem. Why don't you take Elizabeth to the park? You can sail your new boat on the boat pond."

Sara closed her eyes. Sometimes she wished Mama did something else instead of writing poems. Not that she didn't like Mama's poems. She loved to hear her read them out loud at bedtime, even if she didn't always know what they meant. It was just that poems happened to Mama at the worst times. Sometimes they even made her forget about cooking dinner.

Sara had another wish. She wished Daddy hadn't gone away to live. Daddy always had good ideas. He would know the very best, coolest thing to do on the hottest day of the summer.

Opening her eyes, Sara said, "Okay, Mama, we'll go to the park." But Mama didn't answer. Her fingers were going click-click again on the typewriter keys.

Bump-bump-bump. Sara carried Elizabeth's motorcycle down the stairs. Then she went back up for her boat. And then for Elizabeth. At last they were all on the sidewalk.

Sara walked slowly toward the park. Elizabeth rode ahead, bumping into things and making her ambulance noise. Sara made a face at her. It was too hot for so much noise.

On the corner the ice-cream man stood under a beach umbrella. He was selling lots of ice cream today. Sara handed him the money Mama had given her and bought a chocolate-covered peanut crunch for herself and a raspberry ice for Elizabeth.

"Here, Elizabeth," she said. But Elizabeth wasn't there.

Sara looked up and down the block. No Elizabeth. She looked around the corner. A red motorcycle was riding into the dark lobby of an apartment house.

"Elizabeth!"

By the time Sara got to her, she had peanut crunch dripping down one arm and raspberry ice down the other.

"This isn't the way to the park," she scolded her.

"Ice cream!" said Elizabeth, grabbing the raspberry ice and dripping it all over the apartment-house floor.

Sara dragged her outside and pointed her toward the park again. "Now stay with me," she said.

Sara's ice-cream stick melted faster than she could lick it. Soon there was chocolate on her bathing suit and raspberry ice all over Elizabeth's motorcycle. "Sticky-icky," said Elizabeth. It was too hot for ice cream.

Lots of people were going to the park. The closer they got, the more people there were. Sara heard music too. Something must be happening in the park.

"Horsie!" said Elizabeth.

A policeman on horseback stood at the corner across from the park. Down the street a band came marching. *Oom-pah, oom-pah.*

"Look, Elizabeth, it's a parade."

"Nice horsie," said Elizabeth, and rode her motorcycle right into the crowd of people on the corner.

"Come back here," shouted Sara, running after her.

Elizabeth was standing under the policeman's horse, trying to pat its nose. Sara dragged her away. "Look, Elizabeth, more horsies."

Six men in cowboy hats riding white horses were coming down the street. After them was a float with a palm tree on it. Elizabeth watched with a big happy smile. She loved parades.

Sara liked them too, especially when Daddy was there to boost her up so she could see everything. But today the *oom-pah, oom-pah*s made her ears hurt. The bright sun made her eyes hurt. Sara felt as if she were going to melt just like an ice-cream stick.

She tapped the policeman on his leather boot. "My little sister and I want to go to the park," she said. "Could you cross us?"

"Right after the next float," said the policeman.

Sara reached for Elizabeth's hand. But she wasn't there.

"Oh, no," said Sara. She was really lost this time. How would she ever be able to find her? What would Mama say?

Sara tugged at the policeman's trouser leg. "I lost my sister," she said, trying not to cry.

The policeman leaned over. He lifted Sara high in the air and sat her down in front of him on his horse. "Maybe you can spot her from here," he said.

A policeman's horse was high off the ground. Sara could see far down the street. But Elizabeth was so little. She couldn't see her anywhere.

"Is that your sister?"

Sara looked where he pointed. Behind the very last drummer in the parade, her fat legs pushing hard to keep up, was Elizabeth.

"Oh, yes."

"You wait right here," said the policeman, lifting Sara down.

In a minute he was back with Elizabeth. "I'm going to take you two across to the park right now," he said.

The policeman left them on the path to the boat pond. It seemed a little cooler in the park. A breeze fluttered the tree leaves. And the sun had gone behind a dark cloud.

"Pum-pum-dee-dum," sang Elizabeth, drumming on her motorcycle with a stick.

Sara walked close behind. She wasn't going to lose her again.

At the boat pond Sara lifted Elizabeth off her motorcycle. "Come on, let's sail my boat."

The breeze was making little waves on the water. It had tipped over a big sailboat in the middle of the pond. A boy was trying to reach it with a stick.

"Hurry, Henry," called his mother. "I want to get home before it rains."

Sara looked up at the sky. It was much darker now, and there was a rumble of thunder far away. It *was* going to rain. Just when they finally got to the park. Nothing had gone right this whole sticky-icky awful hot day.

She put Elizabeth back on her motorcycle. "We have to go home now," she told her.

"No!" Elizabeth's face puckered up to cry. "Want to sail boat!"

"We'll sail the boat tomorrow with Daddy. We have to go home before it rains."

Sara walked fast out of the park. Elizabeth followed slowly behind.
"Lizbeth tired. Carry me."

Sara picked her up. But she couldn't carry both Elizabeth and her
motorcycle. She carried the motorcycle and dragged Elizabeth by the
hand.

Grumble, grumble went the thunder in the distance. The sky was
black now, and the breeze turned the tree leaves inside out. Everyone
was hurrying out of the park.

At the corner the policeman was helping people cross. "Hurry home," he said, smiling at Sara. "And don't lose your sister."

The parade was over. The floats and the cowboys were gone. A drummer was covering up his big bass drum so it wouldn't get wet. People carrying picnic baskets and riding bikes and pushing baby carriages were all going home.

Sara pulled Elizabeth along as fast as she could. The thunder was louder and there were little flickers of lightning. "Lizbeth scared," whimpered Elizabeth.

Sara held tight to her hand.

They passed the corner where the ice cream man had been, but he was gone.

Plop. A fat raindrop landed on Sara's head.

And then another. "Rain!" said Elizabeth.

People were putting up umbrellas and ducking under awnings.

Sara saw a doorway and pushed Elizabeth inside. "We'll stay here till it stops raining," she told her.

Crash! came the thunder very loud.

Elizabeth started to cry. "I want Mama."

When Elizabeth cried, Mama always took her on her lap and gave her a big hug. Sara sat down to make a lap. She held her tight. "Sara's here," she said.

And it started raining hard.

It rained and it rained. Sara hugged Elizabeth and watched the drops bouncing off cars and drumming on garbage cans. The thunder stopped crashing and Elizabeth stopped crying. But still it rained.

In the gutter water rushed by like a river. Two boys passed wearing paper bags on their heads to keep dry. A fat man walked along letting himself get wet. Drops of water streamed off his mustache, but he was smiling.

The air was cooler now. It had a fresh new-washed smell. Across the street people were standing in doorways and leaning out of windows. A lady was setting her plants on the fire escape to water them.

Elizabeth pointed at the water in the gutter. "Want to sail boat!" she said, running out into the rain.

"Come back here," cried Sara, going after her. But it was too late. Elizabeth was all wet, and so was she.

The rain streamed down Sara's face and made her feel cool all over. It washed away the sticky-icky awful hot day. She tipped her head back to the sky.

"Look, Elizabeth, I'm having a drink."

But Elizabeth was busy sailing Sara's boat in the gutter. The river of water suddenly swept it away, and Elizabeth went running after it. Sara ran after her.

At the corner the rain had made a puddle almost as big as a pond. The boat was caught on a pile of sticks and leaves. Elizabeth leaned over to reach it. *Splash!* She fell in.

Now she was really wet. Sara fished her out and sat her on the curb. "I'll get the boat."

But Sara couldn't reach it either. At school she was good at jumping. She took a running start. *Splash!* She fell in too.

"Sara swimming!" said Elizabeth.

Sara smiled at her. "We both went swimming after all."

The rain had stopped and the sun was coming out.

Sara picked herself up. "Come on," she said. "Let's go home and tell Mama."

She took Elizabeth's hand and they walked the rest of the way home in the gutter.

Mama was having tea in the big rocking chair by the window.

"Mama!" said Elizabeth, giving her knees a wet hug. "We swimmed!"

"I rode on a policeman's horse," said Sara. "And Elizabeth was in a parade."

She told Mama all about it.

"I finished my poem," said Mama. "And I wrote one 'specially for you about the rain."

"Read it, Mama," said Sara.

So Elizabeth and Sara both climbed into Mama's lap and she didn't even seem to notice how wet they were. The three of them hugged and rocked while Mama read them her poem.

RAIN

Rain came
Whisper soft
Patter-pat
Drip-drop
Muddle-puddle
Telling secrets
On the windowpane.

About the Author

Jean Van Leeuwen grew up in Rutherford, New Jersey, and as a child read everything in sight. After graduating from Syracuse University, she went to work in publishing and was for several years an editor of children's books. She is the author of many books for young readers, including *I Was a 98-Pound Duckling* (Dial) and *The Great Cheese Conspiracy.*

Ms. Van Leeuwen lives in Manhattan with her husband and their two young children.

About the Artist

Martha Alexander has worked in many fields of art including magazine illustration and teaching children's art classes, but now devotes full time to writing and illustrating children's books. Among her many books are *I'll Protect You from the Jungle Beasts,* winner of the 1973 Christopher Award, and *Nobody Asked* Me *If I Wanted a Baby Sister,* selected for the 1972 Children's Book Showcase.

Ms. Alexander lived in Hawaii for many years, but now makes her home in Sag Harbor, New York.

W 13/07

VAN LEEUWEN, J.
TOO HOT FOR ICE CREAM

ABC